Billy the Squid
Rides Again

(A sea-quel!)

by

Colin Dowland

Illustrated by Peter Firmin

You do not need to read this page –
just get on with the book!

First published in 1998 in Great Britain by
Barrington Stoke Ltd, Sandeman House, Trunk's Close,
55 High Street, Edinburgh EH1 1SR
www.barringtonstoke.co.uk

This edition published 2001
Reprinted 2002, 2003, 2004, 2005

ISBN 1-842990-00-4

Printed in Great Britain by Bell & Bain Ltd

Meet The Author – Colin Dowland

What is your favourite animal?
The armadillo
What is your favourite boy's name?
Anything but Colin!
What is your favourite girl's name?
Her name is Ann
What is your favourite food?
Smelly cheese
What is your favourite music?
Jazz, classical or corny
What is your favourite hobby?
D.I.Y

Meet The Illustrator – Peter Firmin

What is your favourite animal?
My Jack Russell dog, Bobbie
What is your favourite boy's name?
Charlie, my Dad's name. We named our first
daughter Charlotte after him as we had no sons.
What is your favourite girl's name?
My wife's name, Joan. I'd better not choose any
others in case they beat me up!
What is your favourite food?
I like seafood, especially sprats
and cockles
What is your favourite music?
We've always had dogs,
so I have to say Bach!
What is your favourite hobby?
Making things – especially toys
that work

For little Freddie
......when you're ready

Contents

The Banks of Thousand Island

Sand Banks

The Whaleway Station

Freshwater City

Thousand Island Bay

Thousand Island

Rockpool Rodeo

Prawn Shop

Reef Ridge

Stables

The Jail

All Soles Church

The Saloon

Sheriff's Office

THE NEW BANK

Store

Driftwood Town

OK Coral

Chapter 1

Driftwood was a little town under the sea in the mid-west, just off the shores of Thousand Island. Its general store was closed for the night and the safe at the New Driftwood Bank was locked up as tightly as a clam.

Along the sand and up into the rocks and reefs at the edge of town, the shutters of the old, wooden houses were closed. Though it was late into the evening, not a single sole was at home. Even the little tiddlers were not yet tucked up in their salty sea-beds.

Instead, the fishfolk of Driftwood were down in the centre of town, clam-packed into the Blue Lagoon Saloon Bar. There was a party going on to celebrate the completion of the new Trans-Aquatic Whaleway.

The doors of the Blue Lagoon Saloon swung open and the sound of Rock 'n' Sole spilled into the street. The shadow of a tall starfish appeared in the doorway and tipped back his hat. He gave a loud burp, sending a bubble of air speeding to the surface of the water.

This was the sheriff of Driftwood Town.

By day he was the defender of the law and a fighter of crime. Tonight, he had drunk the bar dry.

His face was as flushed as a red herring and he was smiling from arm to arm. He staggered down the steps from the saloon. He was so drunk he had to use three of his five legs instead of the usual two.

Out in the main street, the sheriff drifted wonkily towards his office, giggling and singing softly to himself. "See shells she sells on the sheasore ..... nah ..... she shells she sells on the ..... hic!"

He finally stumbled up the steps to the door of his office and looked down at his bunch of keys. There seemed to be double the number that he normally had, so it took him longer than usual to unlock the door.

Once inside his office, he hung up his hat, pulled off his boots and put his water-pistol and fin-cuffs on the desk. He then sank down dizzily onto his bed and began taking off his trousers.

"Looks like I've caught ya with your pants down," growled a gruff voice from out of the shadows.

The sheriff stood up and his trousers fell around his ankles. He stared back into the watery gloom. A pink and crusty creature with a deep scar over its left eye appeared from out of the darkness. It towered over the trembling starfish. It was now holding the sheriff's own water-pistol.

"Put your arms up ..... real slow," the creature snarled. "And don't get cute with me, Sheriff," warned the creature. It raised the water-pistol a little higher. "I mean all *three* of your arms."

"Put these on," it bellowed, tossing the sheriff his own fin-cuffs. "And no fishy business."

The sheriff put the fin-cuffs on two of his arms. "You'll never get away with this," he said waving his only free arm. "Believe me. You can swim, but you can't hide."

"Shut your fishy face, starboy," spat the creature, looping a seaweed rope around the sheriff's third arm and snatching away his bunch of keys. Then, snapping its claws sharply together, it pushed the sheriff backwards into one of the empty cells of the jail.

The creature locked the door of the cell
and then used the other keys to open the
sheriff's box of spare pistols and sticks of
Brine-a-mite.

When its claws were full of weapons, the
creature stood staring at the sheriff tied up
behind the bars. "Well, well. How the tide

has turned," it grinned, throwing the keys well out of reach.

"So long, Sheriff," chuckled the pink and crusty creature. It kicked the door open, ripping it from one of its hinges. "I hope I didn't ruin the party," it laughed, spitting green sea-lime down the front of its jacket. Then the creature flicked its fan-like tail, gave a loud 'Yee-ha,' and darted off into the night.

The sheriff cried out for help. But nobody heard him. The town was still celebrating back at the Blue Lagoon Saloon.

In the cell next to him, the metal bars had been sawn in half and pulled apart. Razor-sharp pieces of pink, crusty shell lay on the sand below.

Quickclaw McClaw, the fastest, toughest, ugliest lobster in the west, had escaped.

Chapter 2

Half a tide's ride from Driftwood Town, out in the deep of Thousand Island Bay, the Rockpool Rodeo was in full swing.

The gate to the rodeo ring was flung wide open. Wild sea-horses, unridden and dangerous, bucked and kicked until their riders were thrown high into the water, landing heavily on the sand.

Fish from all waters of the seven seas had swum in to take part in the tough contest. As usual, it had provided spills and thrills right up to the gills.

Rider after rider had entered the ring. Rider after rider had limped away with battered fins and bruised scales.

Just before low tide, the last rider of the contest took his place in the saddle. His hat was pushed back on his head and along all eight sleeves of his well-worn jacket, tassels rippled with the movement of the waves. He took hold of the reins, squeezed tightly with his legs and slowly nodded to the judges that he was ready.

The gate flew open and the sea-horse kicked and bucked its way out into the centre of the ring. The rider held on, his five arms waving about keeping him perfectly balanced. Again and again the sea-horse bucked. It turned and twisted and whipped round like the wildest wild-west

whirlpool. But still the rider stayed firm in the saddle.

Slowly the kicking grew less and the bucking stopped. It was as if the sea-horse knew it had been beaten. Soon the rider and the sea-horse were trotting around the ring like old friends. As the pair slowed to a stop, the rider dismounted. He plucked a piece of seaweed from his jacket pocket and gave it to the sea-horse, stroking its nose.

This was Billy the Squid.

Quick, smart and more switched on than an electric eel, Billy the Squid was a sea drifter who rode with the tides. If there were troubled waters around, then sure as legs is legs, Billy the Squid's ink-stinct would tell him.

When the contest was over, Billy sat down to catch his breath. Under one arm, he held the winner's trophy, which he

polished with another arm. With a third arm
he flicked pebbles at a row of old tins of tuna.
And with his fourth arm he practised fish
scales on an old mouth-organ.

It was however, what was in his fifth
and sixth arms that interested him the
most. It was a newspaper – *The Daily Scale*.
He had just read a report on the new
Trans-Aquatic Whaleway that was opening
up from Thousand Island to Driftwood Town.
The first train would take all the gold bars
stored in the banks of Thousand Island to a

new, larger and safer bank that had opened up in Driftwood.

This was an interesting enough story, but what caught his eye was further down the page. It was a short report with a small, ugly picture of a lobster in the corner.

The headline read, 'QUICKCLAW McCLAW ESCAPES FROM THE LAW'.

Billy's tentacles twitched. It was he who had put Quickclaw McClaw behind bars. There was no nastier criminal that swam in the sea.

Seeing the two stories together on one page seemed just a bit too fishy. He didn't like it. Not one bit. With Quickclaw McClaw on the loose, no fish was safe. He put the newspaper and the rodeo trophy into his saddlebags, jumped up onto his trusty sea-horse and headed off towards Thousand Island.

Chapter 3

At the whaleway station beside the many banks of Thousand Island, shoals of fish had gathered together for the opening ceremony of the new Trans-Aquatic Whaleway.

A huge, blue whale floated at the front of two train carriages. The chains that hung from its huge fins were anchored to the carriages behind it. Every few moments it puffed out high jets of water from its blowhole.

Stretched in front of the whale, across the tracks, was a ribbon of seaweed tied in a bow.

Behind the whale, the first carriage was packed like sardines with important guests from the banking world.

A second carriage with bars and locked doors was attached behind these. This carriage contained the gold from all of the banks across the island. A security cod in a large, waterproof coat sat on the roof with a water pistol at the ready.

On the station platform, a well-dressed crab with a gold chain around his neck was making a speech. This was the Mayor of Thousand Island. "My fellow fish," began the Mayor, "it gives me great pleasure to introduce our guest of honour here today. She is the dance sensation of the seven seas. The saloon bar high-stepper herself ....."

the most fintastic ..... the absolutely
crabulous ..... Miss Clamity Jane."

There was a huge cheer from the crowds
around the platform. Miss Clamity June
stepped out from behind the rather fat shell
of the excited Mayor and waved two long
and elegant tentacles at the crowd. Six high
heeled boots showed off her six shapely
ankles and six delicate knees, all covered by
black fishnet stockings. These were the legs

19

that made Miss Clamity Jane a superstar octopus.

Fish would swim from all over the sea to catch a glimpse of her famous Sardine Can-Can. There wasn't a saloon in the world that didn't want Clamity Jane as their top attraction. In a few weeks' time she would be joining Buffalo Brill's famous Wild West Show.

Clamity Jane shook the Mayor's claw and kissed him on the cheek making him blush all across his shell. In one of her arms she cradled a small cat-fish which she lovingly stroked. "Why thank you, Mister Mayor," she giggled, giving him a wink and fanning herself with a small clam shell.

Clamity Jane was led down the platform towards the front of the whale where the seaweed ribbon crossed the track. With the help of a friendly cuttlefish, she cut the

ribbon. "May cod bless her and all who trail in her," she announced.

There were more cheers from the local fish and fins clapped wildly. A small, red snapper from *The Daily Scale* took photographs with his clamera.

Clamity Jane then waved to her fans, blew a few kisses and stepped lightly onto the train.

"All aboard," cried the conductor. "Fins clear of the doors please." He then wet his whistle, blew it and with a gentle bump, the carriages began moving slowly along the track. With any luck and with the current behind them, they would arrive in Driftwood before high tide.

Chapter 4

Billy the Squid sat back in his saddle, riding the waves and thinking hard. Something was troubling him, but he couldn't get his suckers around it. A lot of water had gone under the bridge since the last time he had set eyes on Quickclaw McClaw. He needed to get inside the criminal's mind, to think on his twisted wavelength.

But before he had a chance to figure it out, there was a loud explosion that sent shockwaves through the water that made Billy rock sideways in the saddle.

The explosion had come from somewhere ahead of him. He kicked his spurs and headed off in the direction of the blast.

It wasn't difficult to track down the site of the explosion. Billy hit murky waters within a few minutes. Broken shells and splinters of rock floated all around him and it took some time for the water to clear. When at last he could see his tentacles in front of his face, Billy found the site of the explosion straight away. He climbed off his sea-horse and began to inspect the damage.

Right in front of him was a huge hole in the sand about thirty fins wide and fifteen fins deep. Billy knew that there was only one thing that could blow a hole in the sand that big – sticks of highly explosive Brine-a-mite.

And then he discovered something else. Something much, much more finister. At either edge of the enormous hole, twisted and broken, were the newly laid tracks of the Trans-Aquatic Whaleway.

Billy checked the tide. The train would have already left the station at Thousand Island. He knelt down and put his ear to one of the broken tracks. He could feel the vibrations of something heavy approaching from far away. The train would be heading his way at any moment and it would be heading for disaster.

Billy leapt into his saddle, dug his heels into his trusty sea-horse and squidaddled off up the tracks. He had a train to catch.

Chapter 5

Billy had never ridden so fast in all his life. Sand kicked up behind him as he crouched down in the saddle to reduce the water resistance.

From out of the corner of his eye, he could see a moving speck on the horizon over the top of the distant dunes. It was the Driftwood train, travelling full steam ahead and zig-zagging its way down into the valley. If he set off west across the dunes he

could head it off before it went into one of
the tunnels.

Billy raced across the sea-bed, leaping
over rocks, corals and the remains of old
shipwrecks. He galloped closer and closer
until at last he drew alongside the second
carriage that contained the Thousand
Island gold.

With his sea-horse still travelling at
break-neck speed, Billy stood up in the

saddle, held onto his hat and then jumped.
Two of his arms wrapped themselves
around the bars that covered the window.
But there was nothing for his feet to grab
hold of.

For a few seconds, Billy dangled from
the side of the carriage. His two feet and
other trailing tentacles slammed into the
side of the speeding carriage and dragged
along the sand below. Billy shut out the
pain and with one final kick he swung his

legs up onto the tiny platform at the rear of the carriage.

But there was no time to catch his breath. He pulled hard at the handle of the rear door. It was locked and there were no security cods to be seen.

There was no choice. If he couldn't go through the door, he'd have to go over the roof.

Holding on tightly, he climbed up the small ladder next to the rear door and up onto the roof of the carriage. The train was still moving at a terrific speed and he needed all of his tentacles to keep his balance.

Leaning into the water, Billy waded forward, pushing against the current. As he reached the end of the carriage, he looked

down and he could see the sand rushing by
underneath him.

He stepped back, took a big gulp and
ran, throwing himself onto the roof of the
front carriage. He landed with a splat,
tentacles flying in all directions. Then,
sucker by sucker, he crawled forwards on
all eight hands and knees till he had
reached the front of the second carriage.

Billy steadied himself again and began to stand up. But as he raised his head, he just had time to see the steaming whale plunge into a tunnel under the sand. Billy flopped down flat. He was just in time. The darkness of the tunnel surrounded him. He could feel the low roof scraping against the brim of his hat.

As the carriage shot out of the tunnel and into the light once more, Billy could see in the distance the huge hole in the sand where the tracks were broken. He had only a few more seconds before disaster.

He threw himself down between the first carriage and the tail of the huge, blue whale. He pulled hard at the bolt that connected the whale's chains to the rest of the carriages. It seemed to be jammed. He tugged and twisted the bolt with all the strength of his tentacles. But it was no use.

Chapter 6

Billy placed one foot on each side of the carriage bolt. Then with all of his tentacles curled round the top of it, he gave it one last, huge pull. For a moment nothing happened. Then all of a sudden the bolt came free and Billy was sent crashing backwards through the carriage door to the surprise of the stunned fish passengers.

The blue whale steamed on at full speed. It didn't need tracks like the carriages and it swam clean over the broken rails and the enormous hole. It did not even notice that it had come apart from the carriages and their valuable cargo.

At long last the wheels stopped turning and the carriages slowly came to a halt. They were just a fin's length short of the twisted, broken rails of the whaleway tracks. Just a fin's length short of disaster.

Inside the carriage the passengers were getting very hot under the gills.

"What in cod's name is going on here?" shouted the Mayor, getting very crabby. "Who are you? And why have we stopped?"

Billy picked himself up and dusted himself off.

"The name's Billy. Billy the Squid. And there's a whole pack o' trouble up ahead

Mr Mayor," replied Billy. "Looks like somebody didn't want you to make it to Driftwood Town. Take a look outside and see for yourself."

The Mayor stepped sideways out of the door of the carriage and quickly came back in again.

"Holy mackerel," cried the excited Mayor, snapping his claws together. "He's right. The tracks just disappear into a great big hole."

Noisy chattering broke out among the rest of the fish. Miss Clamity Jane stood up and made her way gracefully over to where Billy was standing. "Does this mean, Mr Squid," she whispered, moving even closer to Billy, "that you saved our lives?"

Billy the Squid tipped his hat. "Well ma'am I wouldn't ....."

Clamity Jane clapped two tentacles together and looped one through one of Billy's. "This means you are a hero Billy. And please ..... call me Clammy."

The door of the carriage burst open and the missing security cod appeared, waving a water pistol. "Nobody move a mussel," he shouted. "Everyone stay frozen, fish."

"It's okay, fella," replied Billy, making sure things didn't get out of tentacle. "Nobody's hurt and the Thousand Island gold is still safely on board."

"I said nobody move," repeated the cod even more loudly. "And that includes you, Squid."

Billy was confused. Even his shell-sharp brain couldn't work this one out.

"Nice work, Fingers," snarled a voice from the other end of the carriage.

Everyone turned round in time to see a rope of seaweed loop through the air and over Billy's head, tying his tentacles tightly together. Looming in the doorway at the other end of the rope, was the huge, pink and crusty figure of Quickclaw McClaw.

"Looks like we meet again my inky friend," he roared as Billy tried to struggle free.

Quickclaw McClaw pulled hard on the rope so that they were brought face to face. "Remember me, Squidface? Looks like the boots are on the other feet now. And you're all washed up."

Billy kept his cool. He needed a plan – and he needed it fast.

"Now, let's have everyone off the train and onto the sand," ordered Quickclaw McClaw. "Keep your fins up and no-one will get hurt."

The passengers got up from their seats and began climbing down the steps of the carriage and forming a huddle beside the tracks.

"This is an outrage," snapped the Mayor, as the security cod pushed him forward with the end of his water pistol. "Who do you think you are?"

"I wouldn't go any closer Mister Mayor," Billy warned. "If I'm not mistaken, this here crook is Fingers O'Cod. One of the meanest, deadliest, quickest pickpockets that ever worked these waters of ours."

Fingers O'Cod gave a sickening grin and waved his pistol to move them along.

"And I bet your life," continued Billy, "that he's already picked a few pockets since we've been standing here."

The fish of the carriage began to check their belongings.

"Hey, my wallet's gone," called an old sprat.

"So's mine," said his friend.

"I've lost my pocket watch," said
another.

"And my gold chain's gone too," snapped
the Mayor.

And then Clamity Jane flung her
tentacles high into the air. "And where's my
darling little octo-pussy? Where's my
beautiful, cute, little catfish?"

Fingers O'Cod opened the front of his large coat to reveal a dazzling display of watches and jewellery that dangled from rows of secret pockets. From out of one of the pockets popped the head of a cute, little catfish.

Clamity Jane fainted clean away.

Chapter 7

After a few sniffs of Doc Holliray's smelling sea-salts, Clamity Jane soon came around. Still in tears and worried about her little catfish, she was being consoled by a friendly old sole from Thousand Island Central Bank.

All this time, Quickclaw McClaw was busy loading up a waggon with clawfuls of gold, money and other treasures from the banks of the island.

And as he did so, Fingers O'Cod stood guard over his catch, holding a pistol in one fin and stroking the little catfish with the other.

"If anyone moves," he snarled, holding the pistol to the little pussy's head, "the catfish gets it."

"And don't try any of that inky stuff squidface," bellowed Quickclaw McClaw. He took out a small bottle from under his slimy shell. "I've got myself some ink-stain remover to keep the water clear."

It was a sticky situation for Billy. More sticky than a sticky stick of rock from Stickleback County. His jet of ink was his secret weapon, but he had used it on Quickclaw McClaw before and now the ugly lobster was ready for him. But he had to do something. Tied up or not tied up. He couldn't let them get away with it.

Quickclaw McClaw jumped down from the waggon and scuttled towards the huddle of fish prisoners.

"The gold's all loaded and we're ready to roll, Fingers," he grinned. "I need just one more thing."

The lobster walked over to Clamity Jane and snapped his claws together. "Call me a selfish old shellfish, but I think I'll take the girl too."

And with that, he grabbed one of Clamity's tentacles and dragged her towards the waggon. "Get your claws off me you filthy beast," she screamed and she kicked out with her tentacles. But Quickclaw's grip was too strong.

And then Billy had a plan.

Even though he was tied up tightly, he could just reach into his jacket pocket for his mouth-organ. He pulled it out, put it to his lips and started to play a tune.

Quicklaw McClaw turned and laughed. "If music be the food of love," he chuckled, pulling Clamity Jane a little closer, "then play on, squid, you loser."

But Billy kept on playing his mouth-organ and tapping his feet. Before long the rest of the fish from the carriage were singing along with him too. The singing grew louder and louder and fins started

clapping until Clamity Jane could resist it
no longer and her tentacles began to twitch
in the water.

At first there was no more than a flick
of the ankles, then a flex of the knee, until
she was kicking high in the air to the tune
of the Sardine Can-Can.

Quickclaw McClaw could hold her back
no longer. He lost his grip and she turned

towards him, kicking up sand into his face. The lobster clutched at his blinded eyes and staggered backwards. But she was lost in the rhythm and her dancing was unstoppable. The first tentacle kicked him full under the chin. The next flattened his nose. Then as the music went on she hit the side of his head again and again, until the lobster was lying shell-shocked on the sand, a bruised and battered wreck with dents all over him.

Meanwhile Fingers O'Cod stood with his mouth wide open, hypnotised by the amazing display of high kicking. He was hooked.

The quick-thinking Mayor took a sideways glance, then used his claws to snip the rope that was tied around Billy's tentacles.

Free at last, Billy lunged at Fingers, knocking the pistol out of his fins and onto

the sand. Then with a flash of tentacles,
Billy ripped off the cod's coat, freed the
catfish and found the Mayor's gold chain.
Tentacles turned, twisted and knotted in a
frenzy of action. And then it was all over.
Fingers O'Cod lay on his front with the
Mayor's gold chain tied around his fins.

Billy braced himself to finish off Quickclaw McClaw. But he needn't have worried.

Clamity stood clutching Fingers' pistol in one tentacle. She aimed it at Quickclaw McClaw's head. Another high-heeled tentacle was pushed firmly on the chest of the black and blue and only slightly pink lobster.

"What took you so long, partner?" she said to Billy, as the cute, little catfish rubbed itself around her many legs.

Chapter 8

The blue whale had got all the way to Driftwood Town before realising that its carriages were missing. It rushed to the sheriff's office in panic.

"I don't know what happened, Sheriff," the whale blubbered. "One moment they were behind me and the next they had just disappeared."

Without waiting to hear any more blubbering and whaling, the sheriff set off back down the tracks to investigate.

When at last he arrived at the scene of the crime, all the gold bars had been returned to the second carriage. Quickclaw McClaw and Fingers O'Cod were safely locked away inside it too.

A sawfish and a hammerhead shark were sent for and they set to work mending the broken whaleway tracks. Billy filled in the huge hole by digging with six spades at once.

By high tide, the repairs were complete and the Trans-Aquatic Whaleway set off to finish the journey to Driftwood Town.

When at last the train arrived, over two tides late, everyone in town turned out to greet it. Banners of welcome stretched above the station platform and little nippers from a local crab school waved flags beside the tracks.

The Thousand Island gold was delivered to the New Driftwood Bank under the five-armed guard of the sheriff.

The town got ready for another night of partying.

That night, in honour of the not-so-great train robbery, Clamity Jane agreed to do a special show at the Blue Lagoon Saloon.

The piano tuna sat down and warmed up his fins. The Mayor of Thousand Island side-stepped onto the stage and clapped his claws together loudly. A hush fell over the saloon.

"Townfish of Thousand Island," he began, "I want to thank Clamity Jane from

the bottom of my shell. Without her and Billy the Squid, my beloved island would be a whole lot poorer this evening. So let's put our fins together for the first lady of the deep, the Quickclaw kicker herself ..... Miss ..... Clamity ..... Jane."

Clamity Jane floated onto the stage. A frilly skirt revealed just a little of her famous tentacles and a wide-brimmed hat was pushed back on her head. In two of her tentacles she held small clams high above her head as she always did when she danced. "This one's for you Billy," she winked, blowing him a kiss bubble across the crowded saloon.

Then the music for the Sardine Can-Can began.

The packed saloon went wild with cheering and whistling as Clamity's tentacles began to kick higher and higher. The music grew louder and faster and her tentacles flashed up and down in a watery blur like scissors gone mad. Above her head, the clams in her other tentacles clicked to the hypnotic beat. Around the saloon, fins clapped and tails thumped until Clamity Jane leapt high up in the water, and landed in a perfect eight way splits to finish.

All the fish in the saloon stood up. They roared their approval and cried out for more.

And on it went, deep into the night until the piano tuna's fins were too sore to play anymore.

And as for Fingers O'Cod, he was locked up in Driftwood jail. In between his fins he held just a needle and thread. Beside him in his cell was an enormous pile of half-finished waterproof jackets. He wouldn't be pinching pockets anymore. He would be stitching them onto the half-finished jackets for the rest of his days.

Quicklaw McClaw didn't go to jail. The sheriff wasn't taking any chances. He was securely locked up too, deep underground, inside the safe at the New Driftwood Bank. Piles of gold and treasures were heaped up all around him. But he would never ever be able to spend any of it.

With the town of Driftwood still enjoying the party, Billy the Squid slipped quietly out of the saloon. He preferred riding to dancing, anytide.

Clamity Jane had invited him to join her at Buffalo Brill's Wild West Show. She sure would be a mighty fine catch for any fish. But Billy didn't like to stay in one place for too long. He liked to be free to follow the currents and ride with the waves.

Arriving at the stables at the far end of town, he reached into his jacket and pulled out a piece of seaweed. He gave it to his trusty sea-horse, loaded up his saddlebags and jumped into the saddle. Billy the Squid headed off into the sea in search of his next adventure.

But he would have to meet up with Clamity Jane again sooner than he thought. For as the sand kicked up behind him, out of the top of one his saddlebags popped the cute, little face of Clamity's catfish.

Who is Barrington Stoke?

Barrington Stoke was a famous and much-loved story-teller. He travelled from village to village carrying a lantern to light his way. He arrived as it grew dark and when the young boys and girls of the village saw the glow of his lantern, they hurried to the central meeting place. They were full of excitement and expectation, for his stories were always wonderful.

Then Barrington Stoke set down his lantern. In the flickering light the listeners were enthralled by his tales of adventure, horror and mystery. He knew exactly what they liked best and he loved telling a good story. And another. And then another. When the lantern burned low and dawn was nearly breaking, he slipped away. He was gone by morning, only to appear the next day in some other village to tell the next story.

Barrington Stoke would like to thank all its readers for commenting on the manuscript before publication and in particular:

Mrs Sandy Agombar
Sean Allen
Emma Brown
Lynne Brown
Elaine Canning
Craig Cochrane
Fiona Devereux
William Dore
Joshua Gale
Chantelle Gay
Sam Gibson

Rosie N. Griffiths
Skyler Hadley
Lawrence Hamill
Darryn Ireland
Karen Kane
Austen Kneller
Jennifer Livingston
Gemma McKay
Daniel Naidu
Antony Pert

Become a Consultant!

Would you like to give us feedback on our titles before they are published? Contact us at the email address below – we'd love to hear from you!

Email: info@barringtonstoke.co.uk
Website: www.barringtonstoke.co.uk

More Colin Dowland titles
from Barrington Stoke

Billy the Squid
ISBN 1-84299-000-4

Have you read the first Billy the Squid story?
Something fishy is going on under the sea.
Can anyone save the town from the claws
of a monster?

Eddie and the Zedlines
ISBN 1-84299-064-0

Do you know why Eddie's pen ran out – of the
room?! Find out, as Eddie and his pen-pals try to
save the school newspaper from closing.

Weevil K. Neevil: Stuntbug
ISBN 1-90226-084-8

What has six legs, two wheels and eats
crackers? The answer is Weevil K. Neevil
when he discovers something amazing inside a
box of cornflakes.

You can order these books directly from our
website at www.barringtonstoke.co.uk